MW00899238

For Benjamin Gardner Miller – BB
To Charles and Samuel – NM

First American Edition, 1998

2 4 6 8 10 9 7 5 3 1

DK Publishing, 95 Madison Avenue, New York, New York 10016

Visit us on the World Wide Web at http://www.dk.com

Text copyright © 1998 Barbara Baumgartner
Illustrations copyright © 1998 Norman Messenger

Library of Congress Cataloging-in-Publication Data

Baumgartner, Barbara.
The gingerbread man / told by Barbara Baumgartner :
illustrated by Norman Messenger.
p.   cm. – (Nursery classics)
Summary: A freshly baked gingerbread man escapes when he is taken out of
the oven and eludes a number of animals until he meets a clever fox.
ISBN 0-7894-2493-2
[1. Folklore.]   I. Messenger, Norman, ill.   I. Title.
III. Series.
PZ8.1.B345Gi   1998   97–33386
398.21–dc21   CIP
[E]   AC

Color reproduction by Dot Gradations
Printed and bound by Tien Wah Press, Singapore

The Gingerbread Man

TOLD BY BARBARA BAUMGARTNER
ILLUSTRATED BY NORMAN MESSENGER

A DK INK BOOK
DK PUBLISHING, INC.

ONE DAY GRANDMA

was baking gingerbread cookies. She said, "I will bake a little Gingerbread Man!"

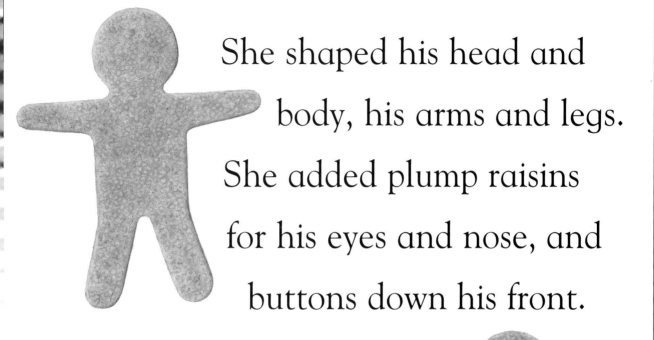

She shaped his head and body, his arms and legs. She added plump raisins for his eyes and nose, and buttons down his front. She used little candies for his mouth. Then she put him in the oven to bake.

When the Gingerbread Man was crisp and brown, Grandma opened the oven door. But the Gingerbread Man jumped out of the oven and

ran out of the door, singing,

"Run, run

As fast as you can!

You can't catch me –

I'm the Gingerbread Man!"

Grandma ran, but the
Gingerbread Man ran faster.

Soon he came to a duck, who said,
"Quack, quack!
Stop, little Gingerbread Man!
I would like to eat you!"

But the Gingerbread Man ran

on, singing,

 "Run, run

   As fast as you can!

    You can't catch me –

     I'm the Gingerbread Man!"

The duck waddled after him, but the Gingerbread Man ran faster.

Soon he came to a cow, who said, "Moo, moo! Stop, little Gingerbread Man! I would like to eat you!"

But the Gingerbread Man
ran on, singing,

"Run, run

  As fast as you can!

    You can't catch me –

    I'm the Gingerbread Man!"

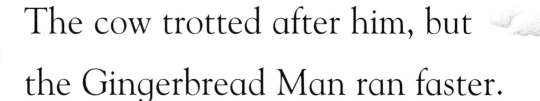

The cow trotted after him, but
the Gingerbread Man ran faster.

Soon he came to a horse, who said,

"*Neigh, neigh!*

Stop, little Gingerbread Man!

I would like to eat you!"

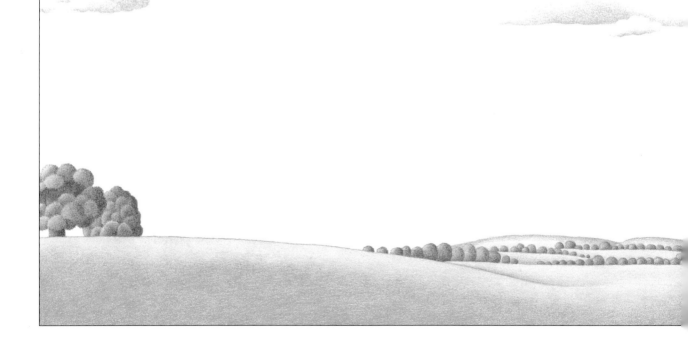

But the Gingerbread Man

ran on, singing,

"Run, run
As fast as you can!
You can't catch me –
I'm the Gingerbread Man!"

The horse galloped after him, but
the Gingerbread Man ran faster.

When the Gingerbread Man looked over his shoulder, he could see everyone running after him.

Grandma called, "STOP! STOP!"

The duck said, "Quack, quack!"

The cow said, "Moo, moo!"

The horse said, "*Neigh, neigh!*"

Then the Gingerbread Man saw a fox

sitting near the river. He sang out,

"Run, run

As fast as you can!

You can't catch me –

I'm the Gingerbread Man!"

The sly fox said,

"Gingerbread Man, I'm your friend.

I will help you cross the river.

Jump on my tail."

The Gingerbread Man jumped on

the fox's tail and the fox swam out

into the river.

Halfway across the river, the fox said, "Gingerbread Man, the water is very deep. Hop on my back so you won't get wet."

The Gingerbread Man hopped on the fox's back.

Then the fox said,
"Gingerbread Man, the water is
even deeper. Hop on my head."

The Gingerbread Man hopped
on the fox's head.
The fox tossed
his head and

Snip, Snap,

he ate up the

Gingerbread Man.

Like every good cookie that ever came out of the oven,
the Gingerbread Man was
ALL GONE!